Wildberry Rose
Going to a Salon has never been this dramatic

By A. L Hathaway

Dedication

To God,

To those who yanked me back, slapping

To those who led me forward, graciously

To the hands I place my confidence in trust

To future shadows who would become to future inspirations

And to those who overcome them that crouch to strike unsuccessfully

-A. L Hathaway

Wildberry Rose
Going to a Salon has never been this dramatic

~.~.~.~.Table Of Contents.~.~.~.~

Prologue: *Ante Meridiem*
Before Midday
Page. 5-14

Chapter One: *Post Meridiem*
After Midday
Page. 15-31

Chapter Two: *Ante MidNocte*
Turquoise Midnight
Page. 32-42

Chapter Three: *Ante MidNocte*
Mushroom Slate
Page. 43-50

Chapter Four: *Ante Nocte*
Olive Teal
Page. 51-56

Epilogue: *Ante Meridiem*
Before Midday
Page. 57-61

Bonus: *Rules Of Wildberry Rose*
Page. 62-66

Notes and Thoughts
Page. 67-100

.~.~.~Prologue~.~.~.
Ante Meridiem
Before Midday

It was about a quarter till 9am. The sun wasn't out to fully blaze the ground and my face with its yellow, afternoon scorches. I rechecked my phone. This was the place. Though I was already dull to the point of boredom, I admit, the salon was more astounding in-person than its web image. It was set in a good area, upscale to the point of pure gold. In other words, a perfection in location for a hairdressing business. From the long-winded staircase, the business gave the appearance of a lux, neo-modern spa peeking down smugly upon me no matter how many steps I moved upward. Despite the nerve in its boldness, the first impression did not disappoint. Regardless, I hoped they had the product I was seeking so I could go in and go out quickly before the afternoon.

Through the gleaming, golden railings, I strolled up those concrete steps to the gilded two-paneled door. From the crystal window, the business seemed to be going slow with only one customer being served by a single beautician. Beside the sinks and hairdryers were shelves of black hair care products: a plethora of moisturizers, multiple shampoos, choices of leave-conditioners, lots of creams and varieties of essential oils. *That* was my target. I was confident that with so many options, they would have the moisturizer tailored for my fragile coil type.

Coming in, feeling the AC wind on my skin in a sanitized dwelling, impressed me even further. The place was squeaky clean, no roaches, no mold. A true rarity in any *"fancy"* salon building I had ventured into. Going in, I questioned, *"Why does this deluxe building have a one star rating?"* Shrug. *"Maybe looks could be deceiving. Oh well, I didn't come all this way to fickle over a little review. I came to retrieve that moisturizer and be out as quickly as possible."* I didn't want the sun to tan my hide with southern heat. Summer was never kind to me, no matter how long I've put up with it over the years. I just wanted to get what I needed and go.

As I browsed the shelves for the moisturizer, a man of about 45 in assumed years, kept *browsing* me as well. I felt uncomfortable, knowing that a stranger was stalking me head-on without fear of confrontation. I kept moving around the store to avoid him but he kept following me as if this was a hide-and-seek game in elementary school. The beautician saw what was going on but did absolutely *nothing* to stop it. It was very annoying, vexing even. I couldn't find what I was searching for, so I decided to just give up and leave before the consolation in my security shrunk to the size of a mustard seed or worse, an amoeba. However, the invasion of personal space seemed all too familiar to this man because he blocked my way with his unclean body odor.

In all my years of living, I had known men to be gazers but only from afar. However, to *actively* **block** me with frontal presence, a crude smile and toxic body stank, was unbearable! The halitosis from his mouth seemed to slither out like sludge through a sewer bar. It was violating that his odor entered my body, all the way to my stomach. I felt like I was in a dirty motel room centered on a city trash pit. The gall of anyone smelling like a constipated pig and *not* be homeless was inexcusable!

"Hey girl, you lookin good." He had the charm of a skunk.

I, to his disappointment, was not for it, "Thank you, sir, please move, I have to go."

"Wait a minute," he swerved closely than before, caging me, "Whatchu doin tonight?"

I had to take a three second pause to keep my gentle patience, "I don't want to talk to you, sir. Please move."

He smirked in a way that boys do when the teacher asked for their unfinished homework, "I'm being nice to you. Don't act like a bi--"

Suddenly, someone shouts a name, his name I assume. Whomever did it, closed the gate of hell but the sulfur still affected me. A minute of this silent encounter made me nauseous until the beautician confronted the man, kicked him out the store to never return and provided me with excellent service where I got that product and I left happy, knowing that an angel was going to strike down that dumpster with mouthwash and bleach and wreak havoc on that stinkbug. I apologize; let me scratch that with the truth: A minute of this silent encounter made me nauseous until the beautician confronted the man, kicked him out the store to never return and provided me with excellent service

~~where I got that product and I left happy, knowing that an angel was going to strike down that dumpster with mouthwash and bleach and wreak havoc on that stinkbug~~ called to *me*.

"Hey!" She marched directly towards me, stomping like a rash soldier, "Don't be flirtin with my man!"

I skimmed around. I could had sworn I heard someone open the hell gates again. Once the gates were fully open, I knew that *I* was the one in trouble.

"I don't want your man." I replied, stunned that she thought I wanted the doody in the toilet, "I don't even know him."

She placed her hand on her hip as if to signify her authority, "Then why was he *followin* you? Why was he *lookin* at you?" she jumped at me so far, I could have sworn she almost reached the tip-top summit point of my nose, "Why was you two *talkin*?"

I thought for a moment, *"You clearly saw him stalking me around the store, confronting me and blocking my way out when I clearly didn't want to be near him...and you're worried about me talking to him and this man is your man?"* I inspected her, she still had her hands on her hips, *"Oh boy, the force of low self-esteem is strong in this one. Where's the anti-force when you need it?"*

The guy ended the silence, "Babe, calm down. *Chill*." He moved out of my way (FINALLY!) and blocked her from possibly injuring me, "I just like what I see, I'll stop."

"Wish you would!" She snapped, jumping at him, "You already have three baby mommas, I can't handle anymore drama!"

I rolled my eyes, *"And you're desperate to keep him?"*

I saw her customer leave without paying. She was not for it either. *Sigh*. I was not in the mood for drama this morning. This woman needed to redirect her priorities *and* standards. If she wanted to keep a cheating circus of walking bacteria around, then more power to her but *please*, it was not worth fighting over, especially when she was the only one who wanted him.

"Don't worry," I said, strutting towards the entrance, "I don't deal with baby daddies. It makes life *less* stressful."

She scoffed, "Oh really? A *tramp* (let's keep it PG) like you must be lonely with a kid. I feel so sorry for you!"

"Nope." I responded, staring at that bump in her stomach, "No kids, happily single and college educated. I don't mess around with baby daddies or any dirty boys."

She got heated, "Oh you think you're better, huh?" She stomped in a fury, "Huh, little girl?" She took off her earrings, "You wanna fight?"

He held her back, "Yo Kiki CHILL!!!"

I stood my ground. I was not worried about escaping anymore. I was not fit to fight something this…how do you say it, "not *worthy* of my **time**. Not *worthy* of my **attention**." I knew that *one* hit, one itty bitty hit, would mean her losing her job and me suing the company for money and pressing assault charges. Now, I didn't like being hit. I didn't like giving hits, *especially* if the woman was clearly pregnant but one bruised cheek would mean thousands of dollars in compensation. No business would ever want to deal with such scandal, even in the upper parts of town. I was surprised how she didn't consider these consequences, already prepared to fight over words. Oddly enough, the boyfriend had more sense than her. Now that really stunk.

Then, as if heaven sent an archangel to a million demons, another woman, prim and proper, came out, marching towards the girl (and not me, thank goodness). When the girl saw her, she doubled down. I guess I found the manager or, more or less, she found me. One sight at her and the guy was gone, out the doors and onto the road as if he were wind itself. I wanted someone would follow him and bring a crusade of mouthwash and bleach with them because WOW that landfill was unholy! The manager yanked her into an office, door slammed shut. Though the door was closed, I could hear everything; the manager barking at her, the girl cussing up storms so vile I wouldn't even put it in dialogue (again, let's keep it PG).

When I heard, "I'm not putting up with this anymore! If you don't stop bringing him around, you will be fired. *You can't fire me! I'm the sister of*—I don't care *who* you're kin to. I know her better than you do and I am sure she will have my back in sending you back out in the streets!" I thought, *"Wow, a boss who knows how to handle her business. I think this salon earned another star."* After that hurricane of contention, the lady and the girl came out.

Fixing her hair and regaining a polite demeanor, the manager confronted me gently, "I apologize," she tried to keep her growl hushed, "She just got back with her boyfriend." The lady turned to the girl, "Kiki if you gonna be startin mess then I'm gonna need you to pack your things and leave."

When the lady turned her back, the girl jumped at her. Why do that? She was literally a mouse compared to her manager's lion. I guess maturity was still waiting for her because childhood never ended. I felt sorry for the baby in her bump because that child would probably have to deal with the mother's behavior and the deplorable rolling stone of a father, who was never taught the absolute powerful importance of regular common hygiene practices. Imagine dealing with *that* for the rest of your life. Future empathy granted.

Without wanting any more trouble, I turned, "Forget the moisturizer. I'll be leaving."

"Wait!" the lady spouted, hoping I would stop in my tracks, "Do you need something, your hair done perhaps?" she asked, wanting adequate business.

"Keep it." I said, striding away, "I don't want to use my credit card here. If this is what regular customers have to go through, then you deserve that one star."

Without any other words, I paced out. I should have continued on but the last words, **"YOU'RE FIRED!!!"** made me stop. I was a certain distance away from the door, so I only heard muffles unless someone was yelling. Gee, what an…*interesting* day. Losing an upscale job position, as well as the pay to match it, all because she was afraid to lose her unfaithful man, that's bad luck. I went to my car, putting it in drive until a knock on my window sounded. It was the little fired girl herself.

I noticed the sudden sweetness in her voice, "*Hey*. I'm *sorry*." She beamed as if we were long lost high school friends, "I'm just too stressed. He's a cheater, you know."

Common sense would warn anyone when a dove starts hissing out friendly words, forked tongued included, a red flag the size of Jupitar could not be unseen. I wasn't falling for it. The girl's spontaneous niceness was as inauthentic as the raccoon on her head, a three-cent buy. Only an unruliness like hers could afford it.

She knew she couldn't fox me, so she changed her approach, "Tell you what, if you go to--(name of street, city, state and zip code withheld)--you would find two men…"

After giving me directions on what to do, I was, honestly, perked. She had gotten my attention. This interest lit my nonchalant greyness on fire.

She giggled, thinking she caught me naïve in her trap, "You should go. It would be the night of your life."

I knew I shouldn't trust this trouble-making, trouble-causing girl, but why not? I needed a thrashing thrill. I needed a spark. I was a college graduate with no job in my career path, in the same boring job, still in my 20s. I was financially unable to better myself to greater areas because I spent my hard-earned cash paying tuition to avoid taking out loans and risking loan debt. The verdict: a completion of a degree, loan debt free but no job in return. It was a wise decision but in turn, it left my life in the same rut. Therefore, I *needed* some excitement in my life. So why not?

Call it a death wish.

.~.~.~Chapter One~.~.~.
Post Meridiem
After Midday

Was I that stupid? Yes, I *was* that stupid. In the years that I had lived on this earth, I couldn't help but be a glutton for punishment. Life was too boring to not have this drive. I couldn't help my curiosity. The paper Kiki had given me caused my wonder to itch and I needed to scratch it, violently. So there I was, wandering the empty streets of the night, a common pastime, only encouraged me further. I remember coming home late at night, closely towards morning, my attitude prone mother asked me one day.

Why do you walk the streets at night?

And I simply said…

Because the darkness is beautiful.

It's something about the night that makes my psyche soar. With a high psyche, reality could seem so surreal. At times when I couldn't sleep, the nighttime feels like a slow dream. Even the unoccupied streets that I strayed on, it felt like a sleepy daze. The area Kiki told me about was on an overgrown abandoned streetway, lifeless, likeable. So quiet you could hear the streetlamps hum. So relieving from crowds you could sleepwalk and be anywhere you want to be. It would had been perfect if it wasn't for the constant rounds of tinted limousines driving by in the yonder distance.

Usually, any vehicle, especially a black vehicle, with tinted windows, was a sign of trouble. I stepped off the sidewalk and into the underbrush, coming out when the coast was clear. Why were limousines, of all the vehicles to choose from, roaming *this* specific area? It was unusual. Nonetheless, I hurried to search for the entrance written on Kiki's note. I couldn't linger out in the open for too long. I didn't want to attract unwanted suspicion, especially around these parts. Abandoned areas were known to be criminal sanctuaries. I knew this, despite my boldness.

I hiked around for a few more minutes before I surrendered my curiosity to indifference. The longer I searched, the more it wasn't worth it. Now, if there was one thing I hated, it was someone wasting my time. I was no exception. As I was heading home, I heard a door slam at a nearby building. I stopped. If I hadn't been distracted by the passing dark limousines, I would have missed it. I then heard mumbling coming from behind the far bushes. I slowly followed the sound, lurking in all directions, keeping myself unseen. I peeked through the foliage and saw two doorman.

They were dressed in professional wear, tastefully refined and macho at the same time. One could throw me to the moon. The other could sneeze a lamppost on me, no touching required. The light above the door was dim but I could still make out the downward slope leading to a red door behind them. This must be the place Kiki was boasting about. I furthered my distance from the men, creeping out of the brushes when I saw a hidden pathway leading to the entryway. I wouldn't want to appear to them out of the bushes questioning them. That would inspire even more skepticism and possibly an aggressive beat down.

When coming to the doormen from the pathway, I knew I had already brought wrathful eyes, *but* at least I didn't reveal myself out of nowhere, otherwise their distrust of me would have been a lot worse. I had a hunch they didn't want to talk to *this* stranger but I tried anyway. It was worth a shot.

Gaining self-assurance to men who were thrice my size, I politely said, "Excuse me, is this--"

The right doorman interrupted, "I ain't got no money."

I held my temper. I had gotten mush mouth from an insolent insecure pooper scooper. I had also gotten unflattering flirting from her rejected sewage monster. Call me intolerant. Call me impatient. Call me judgmental spoiled but I had about enough attitudes for today. These tough guys didn't appear so tough anymore. More like pro wrestlers faking a tea party, sadly their muscles couldn't hide the upper crust elegance they never had. They should really change their clothes to something more fitting, like a leotard or a dunce hat because last time I checked, I wasn't **asking** for money to begin with.

I regain myself and say the words I memorized on the paper, "I'm here to see a gal named *Wildberry Rose*."

The Left doorman scrutinized, "Oh really?" he crossed his arms, "What's her opposite?"

"A Dusk Blue." I responded with unflinching confidence and slight annoyance.

The doormen, nodded at each other, thus I was allowed access. I was glad they didn't nod too hard, otherwise their hats would have fallen off. Down the ramp to the red door, I was thinking how annoying but oddly interesting that was. With security that suspicious, this place must have had underground connections or at least exclusivity to only known members. I never realized the plush carpet before. It felt so soft. I would hate for it to mold in rain.

In the last step towards the red door, I could already spot a faint light glowing from the next room ahead of me. Opening the door revealed a long hallway barely lit with Edison bulbs and cobblestone flooring. It was like taking an evening saunter down a street alley in Venice. I saw another doorman, not as imposing as the last two, a gentle soul over a stripped door hood. He was suited as a bellhop: rosy attire, cap, white gloves and all. I eased myself a bit. I knew he wouldn't jump to boorish conclusions. I knew exactly how to respond.

I asked him, "Have you seen Wildberry Rose with Dusk Blue anywhere lately?"

He opened the door, "Not since Tuesday evening."

I passed him, not stopping, just cordial. Through that door, I had an awe fashioning sight. What could I say about the lobby? A floral glass table lamp with open petals in gold linings, how elegant. Scarlet dark wall lamps that hung stings of diamonds like pointed tassels, how amusing. Ebony tables with pink marble inlays and a plush top seat. What else in this scenery? Giant vases for giant leaves, a nice verdant touch. An old-timey train station clock in roman numerals, central time of course. Let's see…a large bookshelf built into the walls with sliding transparent doors. Not bad.

I would have had a full intake of the décor if I hadn't noticed the slouching front desk receptionist watching at me. She sat there eying me as a gold plated plaque behind her read:

.~.~.~Rules of Etiquette~.~.~.

No sabotaging the Queen

No fighting

No foul language

Professionalism is always favored

Courtesy is a value

Mind your manners

I looked back at her. She gave me a stank look. From her demeanor, the receptionist would make great associates, actually, *best* associates with those not obeying the plaque. Where was the professionalism? Where was the courtesy? Did she have any manners? One step in the lobby and she was already giving me haughty eyes and attitude. I just got here.

It seemed the only way to perk her interest was to include her into some drama, especially unneeded drama. Yes, drama, the most realistic part of a faux make-believe soap opera. It might actually be the story of her life. Someone this lax in life might be an adversary, just ready to pull a victim into some trouble. My assumptions wouldn't be far off, yet this triggered my instinct whiskers, a gift of the night. Nothing wrong with that. It keeps my adrenaline pumping.

Without explanation, I gave the second password, "Coco Chanel."

Nodding, she handed me the keys, "Here you go, Pastoral Bliss. It would be located on the second lower floor."

Somethings off. It seemed so...*planned*. Without question, I took the keys as she motioned to the waiting elevator boy or, more accurately, a sophisticated old man I should say. He appeared well into his 50s, 60s maybe, very professional in that age. Instead of becoming old and bitter, he perfected his professionalism. He must have had seniority. I wondered if others before me had given him a hard time because of his age. He opened the elevator's gate to let me in.

"Second floor please." I told him, politely.

"Of course, Miss." He nodded before pulling the lever, "Going down."

Though the elevator ride was short, I enjoyed seeing the scratches on the descending concrete walls, while hearing the mechanical gears turning below us. This place must be old fashioned, stuck in history or maybe it was built that way. Why not modernize it? Oh, well. Who was I to judge? Couldn't be fixed if it wasn't broken to begin with.

When we reached the second lower floor, the senior asked me, "If you don't mind me asking you…" he halted.

I eased him, "Ask away."

"I haven't seen you around here before." He opened the gate, "You are very…*new*."

"I am." I approved, "The place looks great, at least the lobby does. I haven't seen the whole place yet," I admitted.

"Yes." He lighted before changing to a more concerning tone, "I don't mean to be intrusive but how did you become aware of this place?"

"Am I not supposed to be here?" I questioned, becoming more aware of his concern.

"By all means no," he brushed off, "I just haven't seen any new faces around here." He tilted his head, "You were invited…*yes*?"

"Yes, I was invited." I kept my words as simple as possible.

He lowered his brow, "If you don't mind me asking again…whom *invited* you?"

Easy. I blabbered and spilled everything. I told him about the salon, the bad service, Kiki, everything. I knew that the old man had an indirect wariness about me. Why not? I was an unwanted guest, at least not to the receptionist. The more I explained, the more he relieved himself of any future worry from the unknown. However, I noted that every time I said Kiki's name, his countenance fell. If I could assume again, I would say that Kiki probably wasn't well liked here either, except for the receptionist. I didn't blame him at all. Kiki wasn't known for her five star mannerisms.

To finish the conversion off, I said, "It was such a random act of kindness, I couldn't pass on such a wonderful deal!"

He seemed completely relaxed now. That was good. If I didn't know any better, my association with Kiki might put me in the spotlight of suspicion. Right now, I was a naïve guest who didn't know anything about this place and for Kiki, I was a *stupid*, *gullible* girl who doesn't know what she had just got herself into. However, it was night, my psyche is still open. I got the punishment I wanted. I came here, so I could see myself out on my own terms, but I wasn't done yet. I was *still* curious.

He led me to my room door. It was titled, "Reserved" on the golden knob. I figured the receptionist had something to do with this. The senior unlocks the door before handing me the room key. He bid me adieu, leaving me alone. Nice old man but now he was under *my* radar, especially the receptionist.

Anyway, one sight at Pastoral Bliss and I was genuinely impressed. Gold painted chairs with red cushion stitched in gold damask patterns. Glass tables, polished, no dust. Upholstery with long tassels. A long lounging chaise. A big circular rug with Victorian floral imagery on a khaki carpet with a bed of plush coverings over it. An exotic shoji divider screen with a cherry blossom style. A beautifully hardwood fireplace that separated the light and the dark to dominate the room with a brilliant orange glow. What's this? Someone had prepared a dress for me as if they *knew* I was coming.

I saw that the dress was beautiful…to a "Kiki" girl. I was not amused with this faux silk. The design of this dress was too revealing, too immodest. A view in this dress would mean the eyes on my chest would be creeping a peak every so often because of the lack of linen. Also, my underwear would be eyeing everyone before I could even bend over. If she expected I'd wear this, she was wrong. I don't wear trash.

I shook the dress a bit to straighten out the wrinkles. What's this? A rock fell to the floor. Well, well. I was mistaken. A piece of dog poo fell on to the floor. What did she expect to happen? I put on the dress and smear myself with dog feces? Dog waste seemed more earnest than her, coming from an animal known for its loyalty. Who knows, maybe she thought it was more of an insult than using her boyfriend's. How disappointing, but also respectful.

Kiki held grudges. How charming to both our likeness, but *please*, be cleverer than *that* if you are going to raise a baby. I wish for the babe to be better in intelligence and cunning. Sorry. How *bitter* of me to be so negative. I should be more positive. Kiki, I look forward to hearing about your happy marriage with whatever-his-name-is.

Regardless, I took the dress and properly burned it in the fireplace. Maybe next time she could offer something a bit…*less* her. As I watch the dress burn, a cherrywood secretary desk, carved in floral design in a nearby dark corner caught my eye. I was surprised I hadn't noticed it before.

I went to it, curious. It didn't have a lock or keyhole, so it was safe to open without hassle. Wait! It wouldn't be *"polite"* to creep around Kiki's reserved room...*Do I even care?* Around the desk I snooped and found posted notes not too well hidden. I took them out and read them.

<u>Note (1)</u>

New Café password:

Turquoise Midnight

Liliac meet Plum

At 12:00am

Another password *and* a Café? This place kept getting better with every found secret. If I could find the Café and enter it with the password, I could see what type of game Kiki was playing. **Wait**. Maybe she *wanted* me to find these notes *or* maybe she isn't too good at hiding things. Is Kiki actually a genius or simply dumb? I read the other notes.

Note (2)
Set plan in motion
before the Queen calls
The Scarlet Ash

Note (3)
Need an alibi
to stay in room

Note (4)
Don't trust Navy Gray

Note (5)
Grocery list:
Buy new hair extensions
Schedule an appointment at the salon
Get hair done
Get nails done
Go to the club with Plum
Meet Bae before Jae gets home
Go to movies with Lilac
Buy new car

Note (6)
Baby formula
Diapers
Clothes
Baby food

Yeah. Stupid. I admitted it though; I love her handwriting, very distinct, very curvaceous. It seemed odd to me that a woman with funky antagonistic moods had such excellent calligraphy. What could she make out of her handwriting? Calligraphy takes skill, someone good at working with their hands. Maybe that's why she did hair. If her boyfriend wasn't too busy stalking me, I would have eventually took notice of her customer's hairdo and had a different opinion of her. Disappointingly, her hands didn't match her mind. Very upsetting. Now that I think about it, if the girl had such beautiful handiwork, why continue with a man who was no good to her in the first place? How would she be like if she wasn't with him? What she could have been if she wasn't with a crummy babydaddy and had a crummy attitude? Things like that might ruin her life, if it hadn't already. Just a thought.

There was a knock at the door. I quickly put the notes back in the desk but something told me to leave the notes out of hiding before closing the hood. I listened to my nightly instinct.

I allowed permission and the elevator man peeked in, "Excuse me, Miss. Are you finding everything well?"

"Yes." I glanced at him, "Yes, I did." I changed my tone, "Excuse me sir, but I was told that there was a Café?" He stood still, "Where can I find it?"

It took him five whole seconds to respond, "It is exclusive to only the Pear members of the class-"

I interrupted, "I was *invited* wasn't I? I was told that there would be food and entertainment. Kiki promised me that."

He chose his words carefully, "*Well* y-yes, but there is an entry password and the password changes every two months. I am afraid I'm not allowed to give you-"

"*Turquoise Midnight.* Correct?" I examined him straight in the eye for a lie. He didn't say anything. I turn my back to him, "I have another question."

"*Yes*, Miss." He was hesitant to answer.

I pointed, "What's in that desk over there?" I saw him peek over at it, "I don't want to be nosy. Even though I was invited, I am in someone *else's* room." I turn myself to him, "I don't want to put any food or valuables where it shouldn't be."

"I don't know Miss." He was now eyeing the desk, "I don't know what the owner of this room would or wouldn't allow."

I shrugged, "Well then, I guess I won't touch it." I stretch my legs, "I'm ready to go."

He snatched his eyes off the desk, "The Café Miss?"

"You know it." I confirmed as I glided past him.

He had no choice *but* to follow.

.~.~.~Chapter Two~.~.~.
Ante MidNocte
Turquoise Midnight

"How are you ending the night?"

"With Turquoise Midnight."

Let's cut to the chase. After securing another password for entry, I was allowed entry into the hidden Café. Going in made my brain dazzle. The Café was in a large, grandeur room with a stage in the middle. There were tables in the back and booths near the stage. The waiters and waitress' came in and out the kitchen doors like busy ants to an anthill.

With a sight like this, I couldn't help but revert to my inner child. I felt like an outcast at a lunchroom. Where could I sit? Who would accept me at their table? Who was a trusting good friend or a gossiping foe? I didn't know these people, so I went to the Café's outskirts, the wine bar.

I was in a colorful awe as I sat at the bar. Wines were placed in glasses lit from within, making the fancy beverages glow. The bartender's suited fitted him well. He was old, just like the elevator man and just as professional. With a white rag, he made those glasses shine like pure crystal. I thought I might buy me a drink. Alas, for an exclusive place such as this, I would not be able to afford this simple luxury. I guess I'll just enjoy the atmosphere instead.

I was quickly taken from my disappointment when I paid close attention to the band on the jazzy lit stage that covered the crew in blue light. The singer sang and the band played in beating rhythm. The sung poetry was a sound meant for intrigue, knowing and emotion. I was so fascinated, the expensive wine immediately became an afterthought.

"Excuse me." I asked the bartender, "What's that band's name?"

"The Cocoa Taupè."

That *wasn't* from the bartender. I twisted my head, spotting another person sitting right next to me.

"…they are called The Cocoa Taupè." She reiterated, "They're an underground Jazz band. Talented but have never gotten a chance to take off yet."

I shook my head at the band, "Interesting name. I hope they do well soon." I then asked her, regarding the café of unfamiliar strangers, "What types of people are here? There sure are a lot of them."

She lifted her sight to the ceiling as if to see a list but then came to a simple conclusion, "Those who need an escape," she waved her hands, viewing the band setting the stage for spoken word, "you know; the no-fighters, the peace-cravers, the chill-sitters, the relax-breathers. You know, being around likeminded people, etcetera, etcetera…"

I grinned, "You must not like to deal with drama then?"

She shook her head, "No. Sadly, *not-dealing-with-drama* it isn't in my profession. I just don't have that luxury." She lets out a laugh for herself before saying, "I prefer not to anyway," She took a glance at me, "You're familiar." That caught me off guard, then she said, "Come to my booth." She got up from her seat, ordering the bartender, "Send drinks to VIP #4."

"Yes, Ma'am," he responded.

She turned to me, "Let's go."

Okay? I followed her through the crowd of conversing patrons. Every sight I had not noticed before upon entry increased my connection to **this** *place*, **this** *Wildberry Rose*; of seeing hanging abstract oil paintings, smelling the culinary food and displayed smelted metal statues. It had its own life in its decorum, imagination and simplistic lux. The more I saw of the large room, the more it didn't feel like a cafeteria anymore. I had almost lost my guide twice thinking about this place. It was hard to not be distracted. This night of motion never seemed to end.

Once the stage was set, the singer of the Cocoa Taupè came out, holding a microphone as the blue light made her darkness glow. The band was absent, except one member playing keys on the piano. Regardless, it was a solo round, a lonesome spoken word. I continued to follow my guide as the Cocoa Taupè singer broke into passionate word.

Walnut *Honeyyyy*
Ice Blue
Aaand
Cruelll

Walnut *Honeyyyy*
A Grape Spice
So
So *niiicce*

Walnut *Honeyyyy*
He drink me down
Newport Blue
So cruel
Blue
...for *yoooou*...

Myyyyyyyyy
Wallllllllll-nut
Hooonnneyyyy

The crowd applauded and so did I. Amazing. We passed the other booths into a closed off area, the **V**ery **I**mportant **P**eople section. This person might have been more important than the other patrons. We sat on the red Venetian style cushions. They were cozier than the rest of the Café's flat wooden chairs.

"What room are you?" She asked.

I was caught off guard again, answering seconds behind, "Pastoral Bliss."

She nods at me, "So I'm above you. Or more accurately a floor *below* your round class."

"What's your room called?" I asked wanting to know myself.

"Black and Gold. Just like me." She said as a matter of fact.

The waiter came over to place freshly baked bread and whipped butter at our booth. They smelt divine. I almost drooled. How indecent.

She turned to me, "Do you like white rum, wine, bourbon?"

I took my eyes off the tasty morsels, "Wine would be good."

"Which one? Garnet Rue? Chocolate Wine? Platinum Black?" She motions towards another waiter, holding a silver plate of three different bottles.

I had to think, "I would rather have a wine that is fruitier with less of an alcoholic aftertaste."

She said to the waiter, "Orchard Gold please" before handing him a 50 dollar tip. I felt **broke**, so broke I couldn't *afford* the air I breathed. The Jazz band started playing smooth fantasia. When she was musically distracted, I mesmerized myself to the newly baked bread set before me.

"Do you want one? Go ahead," she said as she gave her ear back to the music.

I was thankful for that permission. I grabbed one. With the delicate poise of the butter knife, I could smell the spices coming from the butter. That scent caused me to grab another roll. Imagine, if I ate and kept eating these rolls, these were going to be *my* Walnut Honey…to my *weight*. These rolls were ridiculously delicious. You couldn't have just one. The poem may be about heartbreak but mine would be about diabetes and how these calories helped me break the chair.

"**Oh, no.**" She said, "There will be trouble tonight."

"What?" My cheeks were full of fluffy bread.

I rose my gaze from my hungry hypnosis. She seemed concerned. I looked in her direction and saw two professionally suited women. The skin on their bodies were clear and flawless like stainless steel, sleek, velvety, and groomed. Their eyes were slit and austere.

She arose, "The Queen's Consigliere."

"*The Queen's Consigliere?*" I observed them closely, "They look cold. What are their names?"

"Ivory Blue and Ivory White." She said with sudden fear, "*The Silent Killers.*"

All of a sudden she targeted her eyes on something else. Before I could follow her eyes, she snapped her focus back to me, whispering, "That's why they are here."

I leaned closer to her, "Who?"

"The Taints."

Then I saw them. Two conversing women in the corner, in the dark. It was obvious they were in cahoots, friends, ride or die for each other. They seemed very close acquaintances. The shades of purple on their dresses were beautiful but the stylistic presentation was tawdry. It looked like another dress I could throw into the fire. Something about how they stood, how they posed themselves, how they radiated an essence of troublemaking reminded me of someone if it hadn't slipped my mind.

I needed to know, "Who are the Taints?"

She kept her eyes on them, "A gang from the west side of here. They are part of an underground prostitution ring." She took a roll, "I remember getting into a fight with one of the members." She grabbed some butter with her knife, "Crazy _chick_ (let's keep it PG) wanted to start a fight all because her man--a father of _plentiful_ children--couldn't keep his eyes shut off me." A rough bite was taken, chewing like a bulldog until she swallowed, "She jumped at me so hard, I could have sworn she touched my nose." She put the roll down, not seeing fit to eat anymore, "We took our business outside and I tore that _skank_ (again, let's keep it PG) up." She sneered, "You should have seen her crying like a baby. She should be more concerned about her children becoming sex workers, than that druggie."

"Where have I seen that before?" I goofed, "What's her name?"

"Her name was Kilala Kile," I stopped eating, "She was someone in my rank, who wanted to cause trouble." She shook her head, "That's the thing about Kiki, she _talks_ until she gets **popped**."

The realization made me quiver, "How do you know about her?"

She was puzzled, "She is the sister of the Mademoiselle."

"*Mademoiselle?*" I repeated.

"The Boss Mistress of this place." I rose up as she also got up saying, "Didn't you know that?"

A gunshot was heard from below the upstairs. The Jazz band stopped. The Café was silent as a mouse. Another gunshot sounded and then another. The whole room started a panic, a commotion of directionless noise. The person I was with was gone. I couldn't find her anywhere. Ivory Blue shot a gun to the ceiling, instantly everyone was quiet. The sudden loudness of her gun did the trick. Ivory Blue ordered everyone to their rooms. It was mandatory.

Because everyone was crowding in at the same time, it took me more than 30 minutes to board the elevator. However, this was to my advantage. While everyone was distracted, I took about 4 roll baskets with me. No one was eating them, so I helped myself. As I ventured down the hallway, I saw women with gun holsters and knives. They all stood by each room door, wearing bright red clothing.

When I came to Kiki's room, the woman at the door halted me.

"Ma'am!" her voice was demanding, "that basket belongs to the café. You're not allowed to take it with you."

I thought for a moment. I nodded in agreement. Rules were rules. I took the rolls out, putting them in my shirt like a cradle. They were still warm. I gave her the basket.

She could take the basket, **but I'm eating these rolls.**

Chapter Three

Ante MidNocte
Mushroom Slate

"Can I go *anywhere*?"

"I am sorry, Ma'am." The door muffled her voice a bit, but I could still make out what she said, "The Mademoiselle has ordered a state of emergency. You must stay in your assigned room."

Great, just great! One hour I was stuffing my face fat with classy music surrounding me to being I stuck in a room for the rest of the night. At least the room I stayed in was nice, but then it got nerve-wrecking knowing Kiki had been in it. Despite my complaints, I couldn't help but think, *"I thought this place didn't put up with this type of drama? Did Kiki have something to do with this?"* That's a dumb thing to think about, *of course* she did, I read the notes! The notes. I looked over at the desk. Before I could do more snooping around the room again, I heard a commotion outside my door.

"Everyone of all classes have been ordered to-"

"I came in the permission of the Queen."

"...Of course. My apologies. Please enter."

The woman from the Café came in, holding a medallion.

She switched from an authority figure to a friend, "I'm glad you're okay."

In relief, I sighed, "I'm fine."

"They didn't hurt you, did they? Can you-" something caught her eye, "Are those rolls from the Café?"

"No. No." I said, acting aloof, "They're decoration for the room, amazing candles."

She held her laughter in, *"Right"* taking a roll and eating it. When done, she sighed, staring at me, "You never change."

That reminded me, "You said I looked familiar." I was leery, "Did we meet before?"

"Maybe," she bit the roll and swallowed, "maybe *not*."

Ambiguity is never told in a straight manner, so I asked her "…Why are you here?"

"To inform you." She plotted on the bed, "Taint members had been captured and dealt with." She ate another roll, "They say *you* were the one who tried to assassinate the Queen." She smirked, "They said *you* were the plotter, hiding in the room."

"*Me?*" I said, almost—*almost*—in disbelief.

"Yes," she smiled, "That would have been true…" she chuckled to herself, "If you had remained in the room." she made a sigh of relief, "Because you were in the Café with me, you had in alibi." She jumped off the bed and went over to the fireplace; "I was able to vouch for you."

That was good and all but I wanted to know something, "Tell me more about Mademoiselle's sister."

She gave me a look, "What do you *want* to know?"

"Everything." I said with a straight face. No ambiguity here.

She was quiet. She seemed to trust me enough, so she started, "Kiki and the Mademoiselle are sisters but not close ones." I took a seat on the chaise because I knew this was going to be interesting, no popcorn needed, "Kiki had a relationship with her current Bae before she became his next babymomma. Mademoiselle didn't approve because he was involved in the city's drug ring and he wanted to level up to the prostitution ring as well for more money." I rolled my eyes, maybe Kiki would have acted better if her man didn't smell so bad, "The Mademoiselle didn't want to be involved in illegal activities, but Kiki did because it was was fast money. However, without the Mademoiselle's support, Kiki wasn't allowed to conduct business on her property."

"Why?" I asked, aloof, making myself cozy on the chaise.

"Because the Mademoiselle is sole owner of this establishment and many others." She further said, "I'm sure when you came here, it was empty and isolated wasn't it?

"Yes," I agreed, remembering the solitude I felt coming here.

She gazed out through the fogginess of the cold painted window, "All these abandoned buildings are owned by her and considered private property. Private businesses are only conducted within the premises." She clenched her fists, "This location is outside the city's borders but within the city limits. It would be the perfect hub to conduct illicit activities. Kiki's Bae is desperate to have it."

"And Kiki wants to give it to him?" I said, expecting an obvious answer.

She didn't respond. I didn't even think she heard me. She seemed to be deep in thought about what to say next. As she was thinking, I was deep in thought as well. This property would be the perfect hub to conduct illicit activities. Coming here was complicated, unless someone, who had already known the true secrets of the area, was there to direct you.

Plus, who would know that a bunch of unwanted, abandoned buildings, that had probably seen better days in its lifetime, had an exclusive membership below the surface level. Imagine a stranger, or the police, walking around the area, not knowing that a whole secret society was underneath them, much less in the basement. Also, invading upon private property with private security would be common sense that one is trespassing if someone didn't tell you where to go. Law enforcement would have to go through hoops just to be granted permission to investigate. If they are granted permission, they would be looking in the wrong place, *or* the wrong surface level.

After a while, she finally spoke, "Kiki has been under suspicion for quite some time but this takes the cake." She went from the window back to the fireplace to feel its warmth.

"Is Kiki desperate enough to kill her own sister just to please her man?" I asked.

She glared at the possibility, "Ride or die, for her Bae."

I got up sighing, "This is crazy."

Her positivity increased faintly, "Crazy enough to drag you in too. I agree, this is crazy." She viewed her medallion, "You know what's funny?"

"What?" I stretched across the chaise, hearing bones pop.

"I grew up around them. I can't help but gawk at them now: Mademoiselle, married to a successful businessman and Kiki is the babymomma of an ex convict." She holds the metal signet fondly, "Yet, Mademoiselle still had the compassion to give Kiki a job at her Salon. She never had to use lethal force until now." She then squeezed the medallion like a neck, "Stupid Kiki, always messing up good things." She jeered as if into acceptance, **"She is the spit on a cheesecake."**

I thought for a minute, "That *is* funny."

It *was* funny. *The spit on a cheesecake.* Hilarious but it wasn't enough to unnerve me. That, *jeer*, that *smile* seemed…seemed…*very* deadly and very *familiar*.

"CONSIGLIERE, OPEN UP!"

This interruption surprised me. This was going by too fast. If that is Ivory White and Ivory Blue this could mean trouble.

She made her presence known, "*I* am a Marquis. *I* will open the door."

"Do so." They waited.

Once the door was opened, they rushed past her. They were so swift I only had a second to react.

Ivory White held me at gunpoint, "Hands up!"

She kept her cool, "This isn't necessary."

"The Queen wants her." Ivory White said, keeping her eyes on me.

"Spread your legs." Ivory Blue ordered. She pated me down thoroughly, "No weapons." She said to Ivory White, "All clear."

Ivory White nudged me with her gun, "We don't know how you got in but we will soon find out."

"You're coming with us," Ivory Blue gave me a look, "Mind your manners."

She stepped forward, "Am I allowed to go as well?"

"This is out of your jurisdiction." Ivory Blue said, taking out a blindfold.

She turned to me, "I will wait for you."

Ivory White glared, "*That* won't be necessary."

She glared back, "I will hear that from the Queen." I saw the fire within her, "I know what I *can* and *can't* do."

Without another statement, my eyes were covered. I did not move. Compliance was required and I knew that. I couldn't see but I could tell that I was led out the door. The hallway sounded quiet. All I could hear were my footsteps. I could almost hear my heartbeat with every step. We traveled for some time. Ivory White's gun was constantly on my back. It was cold, ready to feel my warm blood. We then stopped. I heard a wall being hit. Then, maybe, something behind it unlocks. A hidden door? A hidden wall? A hidden elevator? I didn't know.

Ivory Blue whispers in my ear, **"Mind your manners."**

.~.~.~Chapter Four~.~.~.
Ante Nocte
Olive Teal

I took one last step, almost tripping when they suddenly stopped me. Once the blindfold was removed, I realized I was in a room, another room, *hidden* room. There were no windows, no entries. It was like an annex of the building, except it wasn't supposed to be known. I came here without knowing how to get here and if I leave out alive, I might be blindfolded again, not knowing how to return back.

The room was dark, very dark, a shadow in every corner that wasn't near the green jaded fireplace. I saw figures moving in the corners. If I could assume, multiple guards were in those shadows, ready, prepared to strike, deadly, like ninjas. This room seemed to be a regular office, an exclusive cabinet with ground to ceiling bookshelves, kept records and documentation for professional dealings. The only thing that stood out was the rug beneath me that had the same design like that medallion. I continued to spectate my new environment until I noticed a faint squeaking sound adjacent from my blind sight.

In front of me was an older woman, sitting. She was fit and her clothing was chic, a self-pampered diva but in a good way. However, she was dangerous as well. Her face was unbothered and not easily amused in any and every direction. Her eyes were stern, commanding as if she conducted business with anyone just by eye contact. Her hands seemed delicate but I knew those hands could give whiplash before a sore cheek. Her mouth held no boastful glee of superiority in this room, despite being secured by armed guards. It was then I understood. Before me was the *Donna* herself, the *Mademoiselle*, the **Queen** of Wildberry Rose.

She moved around in her chair as if she were swinging in her thoughts, "Have you come to assassinate me?"

"No," I answered directly.

She raised an eyebrow in mocking unbelief, "*Is that the truth?*" She leaned back in her chair, "Who sent you?"

"I wasn't *sent*," I told her, "I was *invited*." I knew I had to choose my words carefully because the guards were ready to blow my brains at any moment if ordered.

She nodded passively, "The receptionist," the guards brought her in. She was beaten recklessly, hair messy from strife. A gang quarrel. A back alley jump. She was bested, defeated but still held a tough exterior. The Mademoiselle motioned toward the defeated, "Is she with you?"

"No." I said keeping calm, knowing I could be next, "The only association I had with the receptionist was telling her the second code to receive my room key."

She perked with interest as if she had never heard it before. The receptionist's poise shuttered, darted her worried eyes at the Mademoiselle as the Donna said, "What second code?"

I was blunt, "*Coco Chanel.* One of the codes to get the room key."

She stood up from her chair, "*Who* told you that code?"

"Some girl named Kiki at the Salon behind this establishment. She got an attitude and wanted to apologize by sending me here." I took out the paper, "This place was worth it."

"What is that?" she questioned. She nodded to Ivory White. Ivory White nodded back before coming towards me. She held out her hand for the paper.

As Ivory White obeyed, I added, "This is what I was given in order for me to get in."

When Ivory White investigated the paper, she rolled her eyes, "Yep," she pointed to what was written, "That's her handwriting. Navy Gray was right."

"She's being shady again." Ivory Blue whispered.

"This time she's gone too far." Ivory White said with frustration.

By this time, I already knew I had escaped trouble. I needed to solidify my ignorance, so I asked, "What is it? What's going on?"

The women glowered at me.

The Mademoiselle glanced at me from the paper, "You've been set up."

I knew it but asked, "What? I don't understand."

"You don't have to. You were just a pawn," Ivory Blue informed.

 The Mademoiselle rested in her chair again. She chuckled to herself, almost in passing expectation.

"I would checkmate her." Ivory White advised, harshly. She then summoned a name, "Navy Gray!"

After five loud footsteps, I was surprised to see the elevator man slide out from the shadows. I was satisfied with myself, knowing that I was right in my mistrust of him.

"I am at your service." He answered.

"Send her back to her room." She turned to Ivory Blue, "Give that traitor her due." She waved her fingers to Ivory White, "Gather the team."

"How many?" Ivory White asked.

The Queen was unmoving, "All of them."

Ivory Blue almost shrieked, "The *whole* Scarlet Ash?"

The Queen's stone eyes fell upon her servant, as if she made a rude jest, **"Did I stutter?"**

This was bad. The elevator man put the blindfold over my eyes. I walked again until I was returned to my room, without a gun to my back (thank goodness). When he left, I checked in the desk. The notes were missing. With an extra room key, I'm sure the old man could have been snooping around. I then heard a team, close to an army, of footsteps running down the hall. When the door knob turned, I was frighten but only for a second. She returned.

"The Scarlet Ash. Are you one of them?" I said.

"No." she answered, "I'm just a member but I have to make this quick. There is going to be a war."

She opened the door a bit to see if anybody was eavesdropping, "I found out what happened. Plum and Lilac was suppose to be a distraction for the Consigliere while Marine Teal tried to murder the Queen unguarded. That was when you came in. You were supposed to be the stranger, the odd one out, so whether Marine Teal succeeded or failed in her mission, you would have taken the fall."

"What will happen? The Scarlet Ash. The War--" I couldn't finish.

She was gone.

.~.~.~Epilogue~.~.~.
Ante Meridiem
Before Midday

It was hard to sleep for the rest of the night. Ivory Blue and Ivory White stood

over me like hawks as I slept, keeping a close eye on me. When I woke up they were

already gone. The morning was here and a tray of breakfast was already set. Whomever

brought the tray in was very quiet. I should know, I'm a light sleeper.

I rose up from the chaise. Yes, the chaise. I'd rather sleep on the couch than

Kiki's bed. Call me stubborn, but I had standards. Anyway, before I could eat, I heard a

knock at the door. When the knob turned, it didn't matter for me to answer the door since

it was so quick.

The elevator man peeked in, "Excuse the intrusion, Miss, but you must be up in

order to have an hour to get ready and leave the primacies."

I didn't bother to glimpse at him, "A pity. I really liked this place."

"If it would please you Miss, a friend of yours vouched for you. It has been

decided that you be excluded for three months as a safety precaution. You can return

when your punishment has ended but the codes will be changed." He said, giving one

last bit of positive good news.

I was taken aback, "You mean, I can come back?"

"Certainly! You have been recommended for a Pear membership, though the Queen preferred you to Round. You have been given the privilege to become an official member of Wildberry Rose."

"Fine with me." I said, hiding my glee of excitement but I had to mind my manners, "Hey, could you tell the Mademoiselle that I'm sorry for the trouble."

"I will be sure to tell her that. You should get ready." He closed the door.

I decided to go ahead and leave early. To my surprise, Ivory Blue and Ivory White were already standing there, waiting to escort me. I knew the drill, so I continued to head to the entrance as they followed behind me.

Before I could peacefully leave, I heard my friend shout my name. She was waiting for me at the entrance ahead of me. Ivory White nodded in approval, so I was able to leave their side without the threat of a gun.

"I am ordered not to say much but I'll keep in contact." She opened her arms as I came closer.

"Yeah." We hugged and went our separate ways.

As Ivory White nudged me, I was released and was led to the entrance with Ivory

Blue already ahead. At this last moment, I *realized* something. I never really caught her

name. Now that I really think about it, she never **told** me. Strange. Oh, well. I'm sure I

will see her again, despite me not knowing her name. Looking back one last time, she

appeared sad to see me go. Then, a shudder went up my spine. That receptionist. She

somewhat looked like me. Chilling if I had been in her position.

As I strolled out onto the concrete of the blue hour morning, I heard a familiar

stance, a sway in attitude behind me and a whiff of garbage. After the door closed on the

screaming couple, I heard a muffled gunshot. It was a shock to me that an exclusive place

full of tranquil intellectuals and professionals, who don't have time for foolishness, would

use violence to keep the Mademoiselle safe. However, if she falls from her thrown, how

would the sanctuary for creativity and peace of mind continue to exist?

Oh well. I got what I paid for. Plus, I could come back in three months. I'm sure

she will provide me the new password…*if* she finds me. Though my memory is foggy,

I'm sure she will. I've never thought that I could indirectly cause so much trouble to such

a great extent in one night. I should have known better if it wasn't for my curiosity. Still,

I couldn't help but find a back door death very fitting for that girl and her *lovely* stead. I

guess someone didn't play their cards right.

Guess you have to play dirty to keep what is favorable.

.~.~.~Fin~.~.~.

.~.~.~ *Bonus* ~.~.~.
Rules Of Wildberry Rose

.~.~.~*Status of Membership*~.~.~.
Access to Rights and Granted Privileges

~.~The Queen~.~
No one is above the Queen
Privileges can be lost or gained

~.~Marquis Class~.~
Free Limousine rides
20% Discounts on rooms, limo rides and Night Bar
Granted ability to buy a room within Wildberry Rose
Has the ear of the Queen for special favors
-Can grant access of entry to outsiders in confirmation of the Queen
-Can pass along new passwords from the Queen

~.~Pear Class~.~
Free parking
10% Discounts on rooms, limo rides and Night Bar
Granted ability to rent a room for about a month with 10% discount
Granted ability for password entry into the Night Bar

~.~Round Class~.~
Access to rent a room for about 3-7 days
Can only be recommend by an affiliate from the Marquis class or above in order to gain membership

It should be known that the Round class is a class of access, that the Pear class is a class of discounts, that the Marquis class is a class of privilege, and that the Queen class is a class of absolute rule. What keeps these statuses in unison is the agreement of mannerisms, politeness, and a dislike for troublemaking.

.~.~.~Rules of Etiquette~.~.~.

No sabotaging the Queen

No fighting

No foul language

Professionalism is always favored

Courtesy is a value

Mind your manners

.~.~.~9 Words of Wisdom~.~.~.

It is wise to not associate yourself with someone who does not compliment you. Special abilities and talents could always be overlooked when in correlation with someone of a negative aspect.

Bad influences corrupt good morals, character and life decisions.

Mind your manners. Attitude is not needed 24/7.

Never put someone in messy situations out of spite.

Let peace be still, *leave* trouble out of it.

Never *overestimate* yourself as well as *underestimate* others. In other words, you are not that smart and they are not that dumb.

Be wary of underground architecture with fireplaces and windows that can see the outside world. Be aware of your surrounds.

Learn to kick people out of your life, especially if it's for the better.

Life is short. Don't make it shorter.

.~.~.~*Spoken Word*~.~.~.

Walnut Honey
An Experience of Words and Heartbreak

Walnut Honey
Ice Blue
And
Cruel

Walnut Honey
A Grape Spice
So
So nice

Walnut Honey
He drink me down
Newport Blue
So cruel
Blue
...for you...

My
Wal-nut
Honey

.~.~.~NOTES and THOUGHTS~.~.~.
What drama has been in your life?